TESSA KRA

The Petsitters Club
Vacation Special

Monkey Puzzle

Illustrated by Jan Lewis

BARRON'S

First edition for the United States, Canada, and the Philippines published by Barron's Educational Series, Inc., 1999.

First published in Great Britain in 1999 by Scholastic Children's Books, Commonwealth House, 1-19 New Oxford Street, London WC1A 1NU, UK
A division of Scholastic Ltd

All inquiries should be addressed to:

Barron's Educational Series, Inc.
250 Wireless Boulevard
Hauppauge, New York 11788
http://www.barronseduc.com

ISBN 0-7641-0737-2

Library of Congress Catalog Card No.: 99-29278

Library of Congress Cataloging-in-Publication Data
Krailing, Tessa, 1935–
        The Petsitters Club vacation special : monkey puzzle / Tessa Krailing ; illustrated by Jan Lewis. — 1st ed.
        p.   cm.
        Summary: The members of the Petsitters Club go on summer vacation to Marsh Farm and help look for a monkey missing from a nearby animal sanctuary.
        ISBN 0-7641-0737-2
        [1. Lost and found possessions Fiction.   2. Monkeys Fiction.
3. Clubs Fiction.]   I. Lewis, Jan, ill.   II. Title.
PZ7.K85855Pe   1999
[Fic]—dc21   99-29278
                                                                         CIP

Printed in United States of America
9 8 7 6 5 4 3 2 1

Chapter 1

Summer Vacation!

At breakfast, Dad said, "We'd better start planning our summer vacation soon."

"Vacation?" Matthew stared at his father. "Where?"

"Anywhere you want," said Dad. "Within reason."

"What do you mean — within reason?" asked Katie.

Mom smiled. "He means not too far away and not too expensive." She poured herself another cup of coffee. "So you can forget about Disneyland."

Katie's face fell. Matthew didn't care too much himself, but he knew how badly his younger sister wanted to visit Disneyland.

"How about spending a week on a farm?" Dad suggested. "You both love animals. There'd be plenty of animals around on a farm."

"And creepy-crawlies?" asked Katie.

"Oh, lots," said Mom. "Spiders everywhere."

Katie brightened. "When can we go?"

"I've got a week's vacation due at the end of July," said Dad. "And you'll be out of school for the summer then, so that seems like a good time.

All right with you, Matthew?"

Matthew didn't answer. He was deep in thought.

"What's the matter?" Mom asked him. "Don't you want to stay on a farm?"

"Yeah, sounds great," he said. "But please could we take Sam with us? She never goes away on vacation. Her dad thinks vacations are boring. He'd rather stay home and work."

Mom and Dad exchanged a look. Dad raised his eyebrows and Mom nodded.

"All right, Matthew. Go ahead and ask her," said Dad.

"If we take Sam, we'll have to take Jovan," Katie pointed out. "He's a Petsitter too. It wouldn't be fair to leave him behind."

Matthew said, "She's right, Dad. Jo might be hurt if we didn't ask him, too."

"Seems like our vacation's being taken over by the Petsitters Club," said Dad with a sigh. "We'd better start looking for a suitable farm."

Matthew jumped up from the table. "They advertise vacations on the Internet. I'll go and look . . ."

"A vacation?" Sam stared at Matthew and Katie. "On a *farm?*"

"Yeah," said Matthew. "We found it on the Internet."

"It's called Marsh Farm," said Katie. "And it's way out in the country, miles from anywhere."

"They've got all sorts of animals," said Matthew. "Sheep and goats and chickens and stuff."

"Any horses?" asked Sam.

"I think so," said Matthew. "They said

in the letter you could go horseback riding if you wanted." He didn't care. He'd lost interest in horses since the time he'd tried to ride like a cowboy and kept falling off. Dogs were much more interesting anyway.

Sam looked torn. "I'd love to go, but if I leave my dad on his own he forgets to eat."

"Where is he?" asked Katie. "Is he in his den?"

"Yes, but he's working. You'd better not —"

Too late. Katie had already knocked on the door and marched in without waiting for an answer.

Matthew and Sam followed her. Sam's father was busy drawing his latest comic strip, the adventures of Matt the Cowboy. He hardly glanced up while Katie explained about the vacation. Every now and then he said, "Mmmm," in a vague sort of way, but he didn't seem to be really listening.

"So can she come with us, please?" asked Katie.

"Mmm," said Sam's father.

"Does that mean mmm-yes or mmm-no?" asked Katie.

He frowned. "On a farm, did you say?"

While Katie told him about Marsh Farm, Matthew tried to see what was happening to Matt the Cowboy. He felt quite proud of having a comic strip named after him, even though the cartoon Matt seemed to do some pretty crazy things. In this particular drawing, it looked as if he was trying to ride an ostrich.

When Katie had finished, Sam's father

said, "Yes, of course she can go. Sounds like a fun idea."

"But Dad, are you sure you'll be all right on your own?" Sam asked anxiously.

"I think I'll survive," he said. "There's just one condition. When you get back, I'll want to hear all about it, every single detail."

"You don't have to wait till I get back," said Sam. "I'll write to you every day."

"Great!" said Katie. "Let's go and ask Jo."

"A vacation on a farm?" Jovan shook his head. "I couldn't leave Hammy."

Jovan was the only Petsitter who had a permanent petsitting job, taking care of a hamster. Hammy really belonged to a girl named Lucy Tripp, but she couldn't keep him at home because he was terrified of her cat, Frankenstein.

"You can bring him with you," said Matthew.

Jovan looked shocked. "To a strange place miles from anywhere? What if he got lost?"

"He won't get lost," said Sam. "He'll be perfectly safe in his cage. Oh, come on, Jo. It'll be cool, the four of us going away on vacation together."

Jovan still looked doubtful.

"The farm's run by a Mr. and Mrs. Parkin," Matthew told him. "And they cater especially to families, so they're used to having kids stay."

"Some of the rooms have got bunk beds," said Katie.

"You and Matthew can share a room, and I'll share with Katie," said Sam.

"Say yes, Jo," Matthew pleaded. "It won't be nearly as much fun if you don't come."

Jovan hesitated, then nodded. "I'll ask my mom."

Chapter 2

Marsh Farm

Jovan zipped up his duffel bag and took a last look around his room. This was the first time he'd ever gone away on a vacation without his parents. It felt strange. Reluctantly, he carried the bag and Hammy's cage downstairs.

"Don't worry, Hammy, it won't be a long trip," he whispered. "And I'll keep you on my lap all the way."

He put his duffel bag down in the hall and went into the living room. "All ready?" asked Mom. "The others should be here any minute now."

"Are you sure you don't mind me going?" he asked. "I mean, I'll stay if you're worried."

"We're not worried," said his father. "After all, Matthew's dad is a policeman. He'll make sure you don't get into trouble."

Mom nodded agreement. "And just think of the fun you'll have, all four Petsitters on a farm together."

Jovan tried to look enthusiastic. Everyone seemed to think that because his father was a vet he should be crazy about animals. That's why the others had asked him to join the Petsitters Club in the first place. But he wasn't crazy about animals at all. Oh, he liked small, friendly ones like Hammy okay. But farm animals meant horses and sheep and cows — or worse still, *bulls*! He had an uncomfortable feeling that this vacation was going to be a disaster.

"Here they are!" said Mom, looking out of the window. "Are you sure you've got everything?"

"Yeah, I'm sure." Reluctantly, Jovan picked up his bag. With a sinking feeling in his stomach he went out to the car, which was one of those big, roomy vans. Matthew's father climbed out of the driver's seat and helped him into the back. The other three Petsitters sat strapped into their seats, grinning at him. Matthew had saved a space for him in the middle.

"Hi, Jo!" said Sam. "Isn't this great?"

"Did you bring Hammy?" asked Katie. "Oh, there he is! Look, I've brought Archie, too." She lifted the lid of a box to show him her pet cockroach.

They drove off. Jovan turned to gaze through the rear window at his parents, who stood waving goodbye from the front door. Would he ever see them again? It felt like he was going away forever.

The first part of the drive was smooth and fast, but as soon as they turned off the highway onto narrow country roads it became much slower. Soon it began to rain heavily, and everyone fell silent. It seemed like hours since they had left home. Would they *ever* arrive at Marsh Farm?

Matthew's dad peered through the swishing windshield wipers. "It must be around here somewhere."

"We're on the right road, I'm sure we are," said Mom, studying the map spread over her knees.

"The countryside looks nice," said Sam in a determinedly cheerful voice. "Very hilly."

"And wet," said Katie.

Jovan said nothing. He lifted the cover of the cage, but all he could see was a lump under the hay. Hammy must have made himself a nest and gone to sleep. Jovan wished he could do the same thing. He felt tired and fed up.

"There!" Matthew pointed to a sign at the side of the road.

Marsh Farm 80 yards on left

"That's a relief!" Mom put the map away. "I was beginning to think it didn't exist."

Dad turned up a long, muddy drive. At the end stood a five-barred gate, and beyond it a house and a cluster of farm buildings.

"I'll open the gate." Matthew unstrapped himself and jumped out.

As they drove into the yard, Sam peered through the rain-streaked window. "There's someone coming out of the front door. But I can't tell if it's a man or a woman . . ."

The figure, draped in a big raincoat and wearing sturdy green boots, came toward them. Dad rolled down his window.

"Welcome to Marsh Farm," said a female voice. "Sorry about the weather.

If you leave the car here, we'll give you a hand with the luggage."

They tumbled out into the rain. A man came out of the house and helped them carry their bags across the yard to a long, low building with rough stone walls. The woman opened the door into a small lobby with a hallway leading off.

"This used to be our milking shed," she told them. "But once we'd decided to sell our dairy herd, it seemed sensible to turn it into guest rooms."

Matthew looked disappointed. "Does that mean you don't have any cows?"

"Not any more. But we have plenty of sheep and geese and hens." She pushed back her rain hat, revealing a cheerful, freckled face. "I'm Annie Parkin, by the way, and this is my husband, Tom."

Mom introduced them, explaining that

Sam and Jovan didn't actually belong to their family but were members of the Petsitters Club.

"I've brought Archie, my cockroach," said Katie, showing her the box. "And Jo's brought the hamster he's petsitting because he couldn't leave him behind. That's what's in the cage."

"He's hiding at the moment," Jovan told Mrs. Parkin, in case she wondered why the cage looked empty. "I don't think he liked the trip much."

Mrs. Parkin smiled. "If you're interested in animals, you must meet our sheepdog, Jessie. She's won prizes at the local sheepdog trials. Tom's very proud of her. Aren't you, Tom?"

Her husband nodded. He was a tall man with a brown face and very blue eyes. "Best dog I ever had," he said gruffly.

Jovan began to feel more cheerful. No cows meant no bulls either. Maybe the vacation wouldn't be so bad after all.

"I'll show you to your rooms," said Mrs. Parkin. "The other family hasn't arrived yet, so you get first choice."

The Petsitters exchanged a look. Other family? Puzzled, they followed Mrs. Parkin along the hallway.

"The first two rooms are doubles," she explained. "The other two have four bunk beds in each."

Mom and Dad chose a large, airy double room with high windows. Mrs. Parkin led the Petsitters farther down the hallway.

Matthew cleared his throat. "Er, did you say there was another family coming?"

"That's right, the Spencer-Browns. Two children, a boy and a girl." She flung open two more doors. "There you are, my dears. I'll leave you to unpack your things."

The Petsitters waited until she had gone. Then Sam said, "I didn't know there was going to be another family. I thought it was going to be just us."

"So did I." Matthew frowned. "And if the parents take the other double room, the kids will have to come in with us. A boy and a girl, she said. That means one extra in each room."

Sam groaned. "That'll ruin everything! It won't be the same if we've got two other kids tagging along."

"Depends how old they are," said Jovan. "They could turn out to be okay."

"I bet they're not!" Katie had gone pink with annoyance. "I bet they're a pair

of softies who are scared of creepy-crawlies."

Matthew sighed. "Come on, let's get unpacked. Which room do you want, Sam?"

"I don't care." She turned into the nearest doorway. "This'll do."

"Okay, Jo and I will take the other one."

Chapter 3

The Spencer-Browns

Sam slung her suitcase onto the nearest bunk and went to look out of the window. All she could see was rain, rain, and more rain. Some summer vacation this was going to be!

And where were the horses? *We've got plenty of sheep and geese and hens*, Mrs. Parkin had said. But she hadn't mentioned horses. Sam's dearest wish was to learn how to ride. She'd already had some lessons at a local riding stable in return for helping muck out the stalls, but that was only on Saturday mornings. She'd really hoped there would be horses at Marsh Farm.

Katie was busy exploring. "Look, we've got a bathroom all to ourselves! There's a closet for our clothes . . . and a little ladder leading to the top bunks. Where do you want to sleep, Sam?"

She turned away from the window. "I don't care."

Katie climbed up the ladder, holding Archie's box. "If you want the other top bunk you'd better grab it quick, before *she* comes."

"She? Oh, you mean the other girl." Sam sat down gloomily on one of the lower bunks. "She can have it if she wants. I'll sleep here."

Katie opened the lid of the box and began a little crooning conversation with her pet cockroach. "How are you feeling, Archie? Did you get car sick? Never mind, we're safe at Marsh Farm . . . and we're going to stay here for one whole week!"

Sam sighed. One whole week sounded like a lifetime.

She opened her suitcase. Before she left home her father had given her six postcards already stamped and addressed, one for each day of the vacation except the day they came home. She wrote on the first one:

Dear Dad.
    Arrived safely. It's raining here. We have to share with another family called the Spencer-Browns. Haven't seen any animals yet
Hope you are well. Don't forget to eat!   Love Sam ⭐☺

By lunch time it had stopped raining. A watery sun came out, and steam rose from the puddles in the yard. Mrs. Parkin showed them to a smaller building that had once been the dairy but was now the guests' dining room. It had a tiled floor, two long wooden tables with benches on either side, and a big old sideboard laden with dishes.

"There's burgers, beans, and French fries," said Mrs. Parkin. "Or cold salmon with salad. For dessert there's fruit and ice cream, home-made bread, and plenty of cheese. Help yourselves."

Sam began to feel happier. Now that it had stopped raining, they would be able to explore. She piled her plate with a hamburger and French fries and sat down beside Matthew. "Maybe they won't come," she said hopefully. "The other family, I mean. Maybe they've changed their minds."

But at that moment they heard a car drive into the yard. Mrs. Parkin rushed out to investigate. Shortly afterwards she returned, looking relieved.

"The Spencer-Browns have arrived," she said. "I've suggested they come over here and have some lunch."

The first to appear was a man with glasses and a worried expression. Behind him came a fair-haired, pretty woman carrying a baby, and finally a girl of about Sam's age. All the grown-ups immediately clustered around to admire the baby.

"His name's Simon, and he's eight months old," Mr. Spencer-Brown said proudly. He added, almost as an afterthought, "And this is our daughter, Clare."

Clare hung back, looking sulky and ill-at-ease. She had long fair hair like her mother, and a small, pursed-up mouth.

The baby began a loud, wailing cry. "Oh, dear." Mrs. Spencer-Brown sounded harassed. "It's been a long trip and I'm afraid he's hungry. Tony, could you get a bottle ready, please?"

"Yes, dear." Her husband immediately left the room.

"Mrs. Parkin didn't tell us the boy was only a baby," whispered Katie.

"Do you think they'll put him in with us?" asked Matthew.

"I hope not," said Jovan. "If he yells like that all night, we won't get any sleep."

"Don't worry," said Sam. "Small babies always sleep with their parents. That means you won't have to share your room after all."

"Lucky things!" said Katie enviously. "I bet we'll have to share with *her*. She looks really stuck-up, as if there's a bad smell under her nose."

"Sssh!" said Sam. "She'll hear . . ."

"No, she won't," said Katie. "Her brother's making too much noise."

As soon as the baby was given a bottle, he began to quiet down. Matthew's mom remarked how cute he looked, which made Mr. and Mrs. Spencer-Brown beam with pride. Soon peace was restored.

After lunch, Mrs. Parkin suggested that Sam and Katie should take Clare to their room. Sam could tell by the look on Clare's face that she hadn't expected to share any more than they had, but — rather surprisingly — she made no objection. If anything, she looked pleased. She got her duffel bag from the car and followed them into the milking shed.

"I've taken one of the top bunks," Katie told her. "And Sam's taken a lower one. So you can sleep up or down, whichever you want."

"I think I'll sleep up." Clare slung her bag onto the other top bunk.

"My dad's a policeman," said Katie. "Jo's dad is a vet, and Sam's dad draws comic strips for a magazine. What does yours do?"

"He's a teacher," said Clare. "And so is my mother."

Katie gasped. "How awful! Do they make you do lots of homework?"

"No way!" Clare sounded scornful. "I hate studying. I prefer sports, especially riding."

"I like riding, too," said Sam, relieved to find that they had something in common.

Clare went on, "I wanted to go riding and camping this summer, but they said we couldn't because of Simon. So we've come to this rotten old farm instead." She unzipped her bag and began taking out her clothes.

"I think we can go horseback riding here," said Sam. "It said so in the letter."

"At a stable, you mean?" Clare sniffed. "I hate riding hacks. At home I have my own pony, Gambol."

Sam was speechless. *Her own pony!* Clare must be the luckiest person in the whole world.

"I've got a cockroach named Archie," said Katie, not to be outdone. "I brought him with me. Would you like to see him?"

"No, thanks," said Clare. "I hate insects."

Katie shot Sam a triumphant look, as if to say *I told you so*!

Sam said quickly, "We belong to a Petsitters Club. That means we take care of other people's pets when they can't take care of them themselves."

"We've taken care of all sorts of different animals," said Katie. "Rats and pigs and even an iguana."

Clare screamed and pressed both hands to her mouth.

"Don't you like iguanas?" asked Katie, puzzled.

Clare pointed at the window. "There's a face . . .!"

Sam and Katie both turned to look. "I can't see anything," said Katie.

"It's gone now." Clare's voice was

hoarse with fear. "But it was horrible, like a tiny little skull with big staring eyes."

"Skulls don't have eyes," Sam pointed out. "You must have imagined it."

Clare shook her head. "No, it was real, I'm sure it was. It was looking straight at me."

Sam went over to the window and peered out. "Well, there's nothing there now. All I can see is a steep hill and some trees."

Clare shivered. "I think maybe I'll sleep down after all. That top bunk's too close to the window."

She looked quite pale. After she had finished unpacking, she went off to find her parents.

"What do you think she saw?" asked Katie in a whisper.

"Nothing," said Sam. "She was probably making it up."

Katie still looked fearful. "It sounded pretty scary, though. I mean, a skull with big staring eyes . . . Do you think it could have been a ghost?"

"Nobody said anything about this place being haunted," Sam said firmly. "Forget it, Katie. Put it right out of your mind."

Chapter 4

Exploring

Matthew climbed up to the top bunk. "I'm glad we don't have to share with that baby," he said, spreading out his sleeping bag.

"So am I," agreed Jovan, who was busy feeding Hammy. "Trouble is, he's right next door, so if he yells we'll still hear him."

Matthew grinned. "We'll have to buy some earplugs."

Suddenly Katie burst in. "Hey, something spooky just happened! That Clare girl saw a ghost."

They both stared at her. "Where?" asked Jovan.

"Outside our bedroom window. Sam said she made it up, but I don't think she did. She looked too scared to be acting." Katie shuddered. "She said it was like a horrible little skull with big staring eyes."

"Sounds more like an alien than a ghost," said Jovan. "Maybe a spaceship just landed nearby."

Katie gasped. "That's even spookier!"

Matthew grinned. "I bet they've come to kidnap us and take us back to their planet. We'd better be careful. Don't talk to any strangers, especially little green men with antennas growing out of their heads."

"Well, you can laugh now!" said Katie indignantly. "But you won't think it's so funny tonight if the ghost comes and haunts you when you're in bed."

Sam appeared in the doorway. "Are you still worrying about that face at the window? I told you to forget it, Katie. Come on, let's go and explore."

"Good idea." Matthew slid quickly down the ladder. Jovan put Hammy back in his cage and closed the door.

It was amazing how different Marsh Farm looked now that the rain had stopped. The late afternoon sun turned the stone walls of the farmhouse a lovely mellow gold, while in the distance the emerald green hills were dotted with sheep.

Everywhere looked fresh and sparkling and full of life.

"There's some geese!" Matthew exclaimed, pointing toward a barn.

"And hens," said Jovan. "Free-range, too. That means we can look for eggs."

"I don't see any horses," said Sam with a sigh.

"Here comes Mr. Parkin," said Katie. "And he's got a dog with him."

To Matthew's delight the dog crossing the yard beside its master was a border collie. "Is that Jessie?" he asked Mr. Parkin.

Mr. Parkin removed the pipe from his mouth. "Her son," he said. "Young 'un, name of Ben."

Matthew bent to pat Ben's head. The collie gave him a quick lick but never took his eyes off his master. "Can he round up sheep like Jessie?" asked Matthew.

"Just started his training," said Mr. Parkin. "Lesson every morning. Want to watch?"

"Yes, please!"

"Be here in the yard, tomorrow, nine o'clock sharp." He put the pipe back in his mouth.

Matthew couldn't believe his luck. He'd often watched those TV programs where dogs rounded up sheep and moved them from one place to another at a single command from the shepherd. Now he was going to learn how it was done.

"Mr. Parkin," said Sam, "I was wondering . . . do you have any horses?"

He shook his head.

"Oh." Sam looked as if she might burst

into tears. "I'd hoped . . . that is, the letter said we could go riding."

"Ah." Mr. Parkin removed his pipe again. "My sister Fran's got some ponies. She lives over there." He waved the pipe vaguely in the direction of the distant hills.

"Does she run a riding stable?" Sam asked.

"Not a stable. Just ponies. Rescued."

Before she could ask any more questions, he set off for the barn, Ben close on his heels.

Sam looked disappointed. "It doesn't sound like a real riding stable. What did he mean — rescued?"

"No idea," said Matthew. "Here's Mrs. Parkin. Why don't you ask her?"

Mrs. Parkin came toward them, carrying a bucket of scraps from the kitchen.

"Everything okay, dears? Weather's cleared up a bit, thank goodness."

Sam said, "Mrs. Parkin, I just asked your husband if there were any horses, and he said his sister had some ponies, but they were rescued. I wondered what he meant."

Mrs. Parkin seemed as chatty as her husband was silent. "Oh, Fran runs an animal sanctuary. She cares for all sorts of creatures — ponies, birds, hedgehogs . . ."

"Creepy-crawlies?" asked Katie.

"I wouldn't be surprised," said Mrs. Parkin. "Fran takes in anything that needs a bit of tender loving care. Devotes her life to them."

" 'Can we go and visit her?" asked Sam.

"Course you can. She lives in one of the old farmhouses down in the valley.

Tomorrow, I'll give her a call and tell her you'd like to come over."

Matthew opened his mouth to say could it please not be in the morning because he was meeting Mr. Parkin and Ben at nine o'clock. But before he had time to speak, Clare Spencer-Brown came racing out of the milking shed toward them.

"Mrs. Parkin, I can't find the TV," she said breathlessly. "Mom and Dad don't have one in their room and there doesn't seem to be one in the dining room either."

"No, there isn't," said Mrs. Parkin calmly. "We don't have a television."

Clare stared at her. "No television?"

"To be honest, we never have time to watch it. And we don't find that our guests have much spare time either."

Clare's face went first white, then red. "But — but that means I'll miss all my favorite shows!"

Mrs. Parkin smiled. "At first, maybe. After a while you won't even give them a second thought. If you come into the house, I'll give you some study cards to look at. They list all the wildlife that you can observe while you're here."

"*Study* cards?" Clare looked disgusted. "I thought this was meant to be a vacation! I didn't come here to do homework. I *hate* homework!" She turned and marched back into the milking shed.

"Oh dear," said Mrs. Parkin. She turned to the Petsitters. "Are you upset there's no television?"

They all assured her they weren't, although privately Matthew's spirits sank at the thought of not being able to watch any baseball. They got the study cards from Mrs. Parkin and stood in the yard, reading them.

"These are really good!" said Jovan. "There's a map showing you where you can find everything."

"It says there's a pond," said Sam. "And woods . . . and a thicket where we should be able to hear a nightingale! Who needs TV?"

Katie said, "That Clare girl hates everything, have you noticed? I wish the alien would hurry up and kidnap her!"

Matthew grinned. But later that night, as he lay on the top bunk in the darkened room, he started thinking about the mysterious face at the window. Had Clare really seen something . . . or only imagined it? And if she *had* seen something, was it an alien . . . or a ghost? Marsh Farm must be at least a hundred years old, which meant it was probably haunted. In fact, the more he thought about it, the more certain he became. This was *exactly* the sort of place you'd expect to see a ghost. It was so quiet, especially at night . . .

Except, when he listened hard, it wasn't really quiet. He could hear strange rustling noises and the cracking of twigs outside the milking shed. He pulled the sleeping bag over his ears to try and shut them out.

Suddenly a commotion started somewhere in the distance, a cackling of geese and the barking of a dog. Matthew sat up with a start. "Jo? Did you hear that?"

No sound from the bunk below.

Uneasily, Matthew settled down again. But the commotion had awakened the baby in the next room. He could hear it wailing through the thin wall. He groaned and pulled up the sleeping bag.

Tomorrow he would definitely buy earplugs!

Chapter 5

The Sanctuary

The next morning, Sam woke early. She sat up and looked at the other two occupied bunks. Katie and Clare still seemed to be sleeping. She slid her feet to the floor and crept to the bathroom.

When she returned, Clare was sitting on the edge of her bunk. "Hi," whispered Sam. "I hope I didn't wake you up."

"I was awake already." Clare pushed her long fair hair out of her eyes. "I've been awake for hours."

"Why couldn't you sleep?" Sam asked curiously. "Was it because of the face at the window?"

Clare went pink. "Of course not! I never even thought about it."

Katie's head appeared over the side of the top bunk. "You don't need to whisper. The sun woke me up. It's shining right in my eyes."

The sun! Sam went to look out of the window. "Looks like it's going to be a nice day."

"Depends what you mean by nice," muttered Clare. "Boring is more like it."

Katie leaned down to peer at her. "Didn't you want to come on this vacation?"

"No, I did not!" said Clare. "I knew this place would turn out to be a dump — and I was right."

She sounded so grumpy that Sam was tempted to ignore her. But it would be impossible to ignore her for the next six days, especially since she was sharing their room. Somehow they had to try and make the best of it.

She put on her most cheerful voice. "Mr. Parkin's sister has some ponies. We're going to see them today. Would you like to come with us?"

For a moment, Clare looked as if she was about to say no. But then she seemed to change her mind. "All right," she said grudgingly. "When are you going?"

"Mrs. Parkin said she'd call this morning to arrange a time." Already Sam was beginning to wish she'd kept quiet. If

Clare came to the sanctuary with them she might be a real drag. She added, "Of course, your parents may want to take you somewhere more exciting . . ."

"Don't worry, they won't." Clare stood up. "They'll be too busy fussing over Simon to pay attention to me." She padded off in her bare feet to the bathroom.

Katie slid down the ladder. "Why did you have to go and say that, Sam? Now we're stuck with her."

Sam tried to find an excuse. "She seemed so miserable. I think she's lonely. After all, we've got each other, but she's only got her baby brother and I don't think he's much fun."

"Well, I think she's a pain. She'll spoil everything." Katie took the lid off Archie's box and fed him a piece of banana.

* * *

At breakfast, there was no sign of the Spencer-Brown family. Mrs. Parkin asked the Petsitters if they had slept well. Matthew said, "Pretty well. I woke up once when the dog barked and the geese started making a noise."

Mrs. Parkin nodded. "So did we. Tom went out to investigate, but he couldn't see anything. It was probably a fox that ran off when it heard him coming."

"It woke the baby," said Matthew.

"Yes, I heard the baby too," said Mom. "It cries quite a lot. I suppose it's teething."

Dad pushed away his empty plate. "What would everyone like to do today? Mrs. Parkin has given me a list of local attractions. There's a restored old village, a butterfly farm, a car museum . . ."

Sam said quickly, "We thought we'd visit Mr. Parkin's sister and see the ponies. Would that be okay?" She looked inquiringly at Mrs. Parkin.

"I'll give her a call right away." Mrs. Parkin went into the hall that led to the kitchen. They could hear her talking on the telephone quite clearly. "Yes, they're particularly interested in the ponies. What? Oh, not again! How long has he been missing? And you don't know where he's gone? That's the trouble with Charlie, he's so small he could be hiding almost anywhere. Have you reported it to anyone? No, well, I suppose he'll come back when he's hungry. He usually does. Would you rather the children didn't come today?"

Sam held her breath.

Then Mrs. Parkin said, "Yes, I'm sure

they would. They're all animal lovers — in fact, they belong to a Petsitters Club. Thanks, Fran."

She came back into the dining room.

"She's expecting you this morning, as soon as you want to go. In fact, she's got a bit of a crisis at the sanctuary so she'd be glad for some help."

Matthew looked awkward. "I said I'd meet Mr. Parkin at nine to watch him training Ben."

"That's all right," said his father. "Sam, Jo and Katie can visit the ponies and you can stay here. You're more of a dog person than a horse person anyway. Meanwhile, your mother and I will walk down to the village. Anything for the post office?"

Sam sped back to the milking shed to get the card she had written to her father. Halfway across the yard she met Clare. "It's all set," she said. "We're going to see the ponies this morning. Can you be ready by nine?"

"I suppose so." Clare sounded bored. "How do we get there?"

"Walk, I guess. It can't be far."

Clare grunted and continued on her way to the dining room. There was still no sign of the rest of her family, which meant she'd have to eat breakfast alone. It must be miserable for her, Sam thought, especially on vacation. No wonder she's so bad-tempered.

Mrs. Parkin told them how to find the sanctuary. "You can't miss it," she said. "When you reach the top of the hill, you'll see a little stream running through the valley. Just follow it till you come to the bridge. The sanctuary's on the other side."

As they walked, Sam tried to make conversation with Clare. She asked her about school and where she lived, but Clare's replies were short and grumpy.

"Are you still worrying about that face at the window?" Sam asked, thinking this might explain her moodiness. "Because I'm sure it wasn't really a ghost. You probably just *thought* you saw something."

"Oh, stop talking about ghosts!" Clare flushed scarlet. "I'm not a bit worried. Anyway, my dad says that people who believe in ghosts are stupid."

Sam wished she'd never mentioned the subject.

"There it is!" said Katie when they reached the top of the hill. "I can see the stream . . . and the bridge . . . and there's a house surrounded by little wooden huts."

"Looks pretty ramshackle," remarked Clare. "Not like a real stable."

"There are some ponies in the field," said Sam.

"And a donkey!" said Jovan. "Come on . . ."

They started down the hill toward the stream. "I wonder why she needs our help?" said Katie.

"It sounds as if someone's gotten lost," said Sam. "Someone small called Charlie, probably her son. I suppose she wants us to help look for him."

They crossed the bridge and went through a double gate into a dusty yard.

A woman came out of the house wearing jeans and a checkered shirt. "Hello, I'm Fran Parkin," she said. She looked much younger than her brother and had untidy red hair scooped back in a ponytail. "You must be the animal lovers Annie told me about."

Sam introduced Jo and Katie and explained about the Petsitters. She added, "And this is Clare. She's not a Petsitter but she loves horses, like me."

Clare was wearing her bad-smell-under-the-nose expression. "We came to see if you've got any horses for hire."

Fran looked puzzled. "Not for hire, no. But you're welcome to ride a couple of the ponies. The problem is —"

"We know," said Jovan. "Your son's gotten lost."

Fran stared at him. "My son?"

"Charlie," said Katie. "We heard Mrs. Parkin talking to you. Would you like us to help you look for him?"

"I'd certainly be glad for some help," said Fran. "But Charlie's not my son. He's a capuchin monkey."

Chapter 6

A Sort of Petsitting Job

"A monkey?" Sam was amazed. "Mrs. Parkin told us you looked after rescued animals, but she didn't mention monkeys."

"She said all sorts of creatures," Katie reminded her.

"Yes, I know . . . but *monkeys*!" Sam couldn't get over it. "I thought she meant just ordinary animals, like donkeys and badgers and foxes. I never expected anything unusual like a monkey."

"Charlie was rescued from an illegal pet trader," Fran explained. "His rescuer brought him to me because she knew I had several capuchins already, and she wanted him to be with his own kind. He was in a terrible state when he arrived — thin and covered with sores. But that was two years ago. Now he's a very fit and active little monkey."

"Why did Mrs. Parkin say 'Oh, not again'?" asked Jovan. "Does he often run away?"

Fran sighed. "This is the third time. The first time I found him up a tree and the second time he was asleep in my bed. But this time he's been missing for nearly twenty-four hours. He's never been gone overnight before."

"He must be getting hungry by now," said Sam. "What will he do for food?"

"Capuchins live mainly on fruit and nuts," said Fran. "But they also eat leaves, birds' eggs, and insects."

"Insects?" Katie looked alarmed. "I hope they don't eat cockroaches!"

Sam explained, "Katie has a pet cockroach named Archie. She's our expert on creepy-crawlies."

"Oh, I see." Fran smiled at her. "Would you like to come and see the other monkeys? Then you'll know what Charlie looks like."

"Yes, please!" said Sam. "I've never seen a monkey before, not a real live one in the flesh."

"Surely you've seen one at a safari park!" Clare said impatiently. "I'd rather go and see the ponies. After all, that's what we came for."

Fran looked surprised. "You can go and see the ponies if you prefer. You'll find them in the paddock with the donkey. But I warn you, one of them is highly nervous and should be approached with care."

"I'm good with ponies," Clare said confidently. "I've got one of my own at home."

"In that case you'll know that all horses should be treated with respect," said Fran.

"Don't worry, I'll be careful." Clare stuck her hands in her jeans pockets and marched off in the direction of the paddock.

"Know-it-all!" Katie muttered as soon as Clare was out of earshot.

Secretly, Sam agreed with her. The truth was, she'd never been to a safari park — but she wasn't going to tell Clare that!

Fran led them around to the back of the house. The monkey enclosure was a large wire cage with a wooden shed for shelter, a tree for climbing, and several ropes and swings. As soon as they saw Fran, three small brown monkeys came rushing toward her, chattering shrilly.

"Oh, they look so cute and cuddly!" exclaimed Sam.

Fran regarded them sadly. "I believe they're as worried about Charlie as I am," she said.

"How did he get out of the cage?" asked Jovan a little nervously, watching the monkeys swarm up and down the wire.

"He wasn't in the cage," said Fran.

"He's so tame that I often carry him around on my shoulder. Yesterday, when I was talking on the telephone, he got bored and went off on his own. He's a very curious little monkey. He loves to explore, and usually I don't worry about him too much. But this time he must have gone farther than usual and gotten lost."

Sam peered at the tiny wizened features of the three monkeys clustered around the door. They looked so human, like little old men. Even though the cage was large, she hated to think of them being shut up for the rest of their lives.

"Will you ever be able to release them back into the wild?" she asked.

Fran shook her head. "They wouldn't stand a chance. They were only babies when they were snatched from their mothers and brought here in crates. The best I can do for them now is let them live as natural a life as possible. It's a poor substitute for the jungles of South America, but at least they're safe." She bit her lip. "Well, fairly safe."

Suddenly one of the monkeys opened his mouth and made a loud barking noise. Everyone jumped.

Fran laughed. "They're very noisy little creatures." Her laughter faded. "That's what's so strange. I stayed awake nearly all last night, but I didn't hear Charlie once. He must either have gone farther away than usual, or . . ." She didn't complete the sentence, but tears came into her eyes.

Sam said quickly, "Don't worry, we'll help you find him. Where should we start looking?"

Fran brushed the tears away. "What I'd

really like you to do is stay close to my office, in case the telephone rings. Then I can go up to the woods and call his name. If he's up a tree, he's far more likely to come to me than he is to you."

Sam hid her disappointment. Of course, it made sense that Fran should be the one to look for Charlie. "You can trust us to take care of the sanctuary for you," she said. "We Petsitters are experts at taking care of other people's animals. That's our job."

Fran thanked them. "I won't be long," she promised.

When she had gone, Jovan said, "It doesn't take three of us to answer the telephone. I'll do it if you want. You can go and join Clare with the ponies."

Sam brightened. "Okay. Come on, Katie."

"I'd rather stay here and watch the monkeys," said Katie.

Sam went straight to the paddock. Inside were three ponies and a donkey. But there was no sign of Clare.

She leaned over the fence. The two smaller ponies, one gray and one brown with a white blaze, came trotting up to greet her. The third pony, a handsome chestnut, watched her warily from a distance. He must be the nervous one Fran had warned them about.

"Hi!" Clare came out of a nearby shed, carrying a saddle and a bridle. She looked unusually cheerful. "It took me ages to find the tack room — and there's hardly anything in there anyway, just a couple of worn-out old saddles. It's nothing like the stable where I keep Gambol at home."

Sam looked at her doubtfully. "Fran's gone to search for Charlie. Don't you think we should wait until she gets back?"

"I don't see why." Clare heaved the saddle onto the fence. "She knows we both came here to ride, so we might as well get on with it. It's not as if we're complete novices."

"I'm still a *bit* of a novice," said Sam. She watched Clare open the gate. "Which one are you going to choose?"

Clare smiled. "Which one do you think?"

"The gray looks quite easy to ride."

"He's *ancient!*" said Clare scornfully. "The fastest he could manage is a gentle trot. I prefer something a bit livelier."

Sam stared at her. "Not the chestnut!"

"Of course the chestnut. He's the only

decent pony here." She shut the gate behind her.

"But he looks so nervous! Remember that Fran said he should be approached with care."

"Don't worry. I know what I'm doing." Clare fumbled in her pocket. "Look, I found a carrot in the shed. This'll make him come to me, just you watch."

Sam watched anxiously as Clare approached the chestnut pony. He started backing away as soon as she came near, tossing his head and rolling his eyes. She spoke to him gently, but he immediately wheeled around and cantered off to the farthest end of the field. Clare pursued him, still holding out the carrot. This time he waited until she had almost reached him, then reared up with a loud whinny, pawing at her with

his hooves. Hastily Clare retreated and the chestnut trotted off, his ears flat against his head.

"Please, leave him alone," Sam begged. "You're frightening him."

Clare looked a little shaken. "He does seem pretty wild. But I'm sure I could tame him if I could only get close enough. I'll just give it one more try . . ."

"No!" Sam climbed onto the gate. "Sorry, Clare, but I won't let you."

Clare turned around to stare at her. "What do you mean, you won't let me?"

"Fran asked us to take care of the sanctuary because she thought she could trust us. It's a sort of petsitting job, really. So that means I'm in charge, and I say you've got to leave that horse alone." Sam stuck out her chin. "Okay?"

For a moment, Clare looked as if she

was going to blow her top. But then, to Sam's relief, she seemed to change her mind. "Okay," she said meekly.

Sam opened the gate for her. "We could still try riding the other two ponies if you want," she offered. "They seem quiet enough."

"Too quiet for me." Clare picked up the saddle from the fence. "I might as well take this back to the shed."

Sam watched her go, surprised that she had given in so easily. Perhaps she had been more frightened than she wanted to admit. The chestnut had looked pretty terrifying when he reared up and pawed at the air.

Suddenly, Clare stopped. She swung around to glare at Sam. "But someday I'm going to tame that pony, just you wait and see!"

Chapter 7

Katie's Worried

Jovan found Fran's office without difficulty. He was glad he'd offered to answer the telephone. Like Sam, he'd been surprised to see the monkeys. But *un*like Sam, he didn't think they were cute and cuddly. He remembered his father once saying that monkeys did NOT make good pets because they could be spiteful. This was the reason he had no interest in joining the search for Charlie. If Charlie didn't want to be recaptured, he might turn out to be very spiteful indeed.

Fran's desk was covered with papers, mainly letters. Jovan discovered a pile of animal care magazines and settled down to read a fascinating article about hamsters.

The telephone rang twice. The first caller was Mrs. Parkin, asking if Fran had found Charlie yet. The second was a woman who had rescued a barn owl with a broken wing and wanted to bring it to the sanctuary. He took her name and number and promised Fran would call her back.

Katie appeared in the doorway. "I want to go home," she announced.

Jovan looked up, startled. "Home?"

"Oh, I don't mean *home* home. I want to go back to Marsh Farm." Her face was white and stiff, as if something had frightened her.

"Why? What's the matter?" asked Jovan.

"Nothing." She pressed her lips together. "If you won't come with me, I'll go alone."

"But we can't leave till Fran gets back . . ."

"It's all right, I'm here." Fran appeared in the doorway behind Katie. "Any messages?"

Jovan told her about the two telephone calls. "Did you find Charlie?" he asked.

Fran shook her head. "I'll have to tell the police," she said sadly. "It's not that he's dangerous, but he could give someone an awful fright."

Katie said insistently, "Come on, Jo. We can go now."

"Oh, all right." He stood up. "But we'll have to tell Sam and Clare first."

"They're outside," said Fran. "I was just talking to them."

They found Sam and Clare leaning against the gate. Sam looked rather grim, Jovan thought, and Clare was sulking.

"Sorry I don't have time to show you all around the place," Fran said. "If you come back tomorrow, I'll try to do it then."

"We'd love to come back," said Sam.

Fran glanced at Clare. "But I'm afraid I still can't let you ride Major. He's wary of strangers — and with good reason. He's been very badly treated in the past. It'll be a long time before he lets anyone ride him again, if ever."

Clare pursed up her mouth but kept silent.

They said goodbye to Fran and set off, Katie leading the way at a fast pace.

"Why is she in such a hurry?" Sam asked Jovan in a low voice.

"I don't know," muttered Jovan. "For some reason, she's desperate to get back to Marsh Farm."

Sam glanced over her shoulder at Clare, who was lagging behind. "I had a bit of trouble with you-know-who," she whispered. "She wanted to ride that horse Fran warned us about."

"You mean the nervous one?"

Sam nodded. "His name's Major. Luckily she couldn't catch him. If we come back tomorrow, we'll have to watch her."

Jovan groaned. "Do you think we're stuck with her for the whole vacation?"

"Looks like it." Sam sighed. "I feel sorry for her in a way, but I wish she didn't act so superior, especially about horses. It really gets on my nerves!"

As soon as they reached the farm, Katie ran ahead, heading straight for the milking shed. Seconds later she came out of the door, smiling with relief. "It's all right," she said. "Archie's safe."

"Well, of course he's safe," said Sam. "What did you think had happened to him?"

Katie shook her head and went back into the shed.

At lunchtime Matthew returned, full of excitement after the morning he'd spent with Mr. Parkin and Ben. "It was amazing!" he said. "If Mr. Parkin says 'Away,' Ben knows he has to move to his left. 'Come by' means go right, and

'Stand' means stop. Soon he'll learn how to obey just a whistle. Then he'll be able to round up the sheep even when Mr. Parkin's far away."

In the afternoon, Matthew's parents took them to visit the car museum. They invited Clare to join them, but she said, "No, thanks. I hate museums." The Petsitters breathed a sigh of relief. But as they drove out of the yard, Jovan saw her watching them with a look of regret on her face.

After dinner, Jovan was lying on his bunk, playing with Hammy, when Sam stuck her head around the door. "Can we come in?" she said. "Katie's got something important to tell you."

She dragged Katie inside without waiting for an answer.

Matthew looked over the edge of the top bunk, where he lay reading a book he had bought at the car museum. "What's wrong?" he asked.

"Nothing's wrong, exactly," said Sam. "Go on, Katie. Tell them what you just told me."

Katie was still holding Archie's box. She had refused to be parted from her pet cockroach ever since the morning. She had even taken him to the museum.

"They'll laugh," she said, looking embarrassed.

"No, they won't." Sam glared forbiddingly at Jovan and Matthew.

Katie said slowly, "Well . . . you know this morning at the sanctuary when the rest of you went off and I stayed behind with the monkeys? I watched them for ages, and they kept reminding me of

something, but I couldn't think what. Then suddenly I did and . . . Promise you won't laugh?"

"Oh, get on with it!" said Matthew impatiently.

"I *am* getting on with it!" snapped Katie. "You remember last night Clare said she saw a ghost, but we said it was more likely an alien because it had a face like a skull and big, big eyes? Well, so do the monkeys!"

"So do the monkeys what?" asked Jovan, stroking Hammy's head.

"Have faces like skulls and big, big eyes."

Matthew whistled through his teeth. "You're saying it could have been Charlie she saw?"

Katie hurried on, "Oh, I know it sounds crazy, but he could have been hanging from the tree outside our window. And then I remembered how Fran said he ate insects and I began to worry about Archie. I knew we'd left the window open and a monkey could easily get inside and lift up the lid of Archie's box . . . and if he was hungry he'd gobble Archie up in no time. That's why I was in such a hurry to get back." She stuck out her chin. "You can laugh now if you want."

Matthew didn't laugh. He said, "But if it was Charlie, why didn't Clare say something when she saw the other monkeys?"

"Because she *didn't* see the other monkeys!" Sam exclaimed. "She went off to look at the ponies instead."

"This is a really long way from the sanctuary," Jovan pointed out. "It took us at least twenty minutes to walk there.

With all the countryside to choose from, why should Charlie come to Marsh Farm?"

"He could have been here before," said Sam. "Fran might have brought him on a visit. And she said that capuchins are intelligent, so maybe he remembered the way."

Matthew said slowly, "Or maybe he got lost, and when he saw the farm he recognized it as a place he knew."

"So that means he could have been hiding here all the time!" said Sam excitedly.

Jovan's heart sank. A game of hide-and-seek with a spiteful monkey was NOT his idea of fun. He put Hammy back in his cage on the table beside his bunk and firmly fastened the door.

"Maybe it wasn't a fox that disturbed

the geese last night," said Matthew. "It could have been Charlie . . ."

"And you said you heard a dog barking," said Katie. "Well, monkeys bark too. We heard them today."

"That settles it," said Matthew. "We'd better start searching right away."

"Don't you think we should let Fran know, first?" said Sam.

"I'll do that," said Jovan quickly. "I'll ask Mrs. Parkin to let me use her phone. The rest of you can start looking."

"Okay, come on," said Sam. "We can't afford to waste a second."

Chapter 8

Looking for Charlie

First, Katie went back to her room to make sure the window was securely shut. She lifted the lid of Archie's box and peered inside. He hissed at her warningly.

"Don't worry, my dear," she murmured. "I won't let you be gobbled up by any bad old monkey . . ."

"Who are you talking to?" asked a voice behind her.

Katie swung around to see Clare lying on her bunk, reading a magazine. "Sorry, I didn't know you were there. Actually, I was talking to my cockroach. Do you want to see him?" She held out the box.

Clare looked inside and shuddered. "I'd rather have something soft and furry that I could cuddle."

Katie replaced the lid. "Don't you have any pets at home?"

"I used to have a rabbit, but it died." Clare's mouth drooped at the corners. "Mom and Dad won't let me have another one. They say it's not hygienic to keep animals when there's a baby around."

Katie said sympathetically, "Never mind, at least we've solved the mystery of your alien."

"My what?"

"Remember the skull with big eyes you saw looking through the window last night?" Katie couldn't help boasting just a little. "Actually, it was me that figured it out. As soon as I saw the other monkeys, I realized it must have been Charlie you saw. If you'd come with us you'd have realized it, too."

Clare stared at her. "The monkey? Here?"

"We think he must have gotten lost and found his way to the farm," Katie explained. "So now we're going to search for him. Do you want to come?"

Clare hesitated. Then she tossed aside the magazine and swung her legs off the bunk. "I suppose it'll be something to do."

Poor Clare, she must have had a really boring afternoon stuck here by herself,

Katie thought. She'd have been much better off coming with them to the car museum.

They met Matthew and Sam outside in the yard. "Clare's come to help," Katie explained. "Where do you want us to start?"

"I'll go up to the woods," said Sam. "Fran said he loves climbing trees. I bet that's where he'll be."

"I'll search the barn," said Matthew. "He could be hiding in the rafters."

"I think we should look behind the milking shed," said Katie. "That's where he was when Clare saw him looking through the window."

"Okay," said Sam. "Matthew can take the barn and I'll take the woods. Katie, you can look behind the milking shed.

And be careful not to make too much noise. We don't want to frighten him."

"What about me?" asked Clare.

Sam sighed. "You can help me search the woods."

At that moment, Jovan raced up. "Fran's coming right over," he panted. "And guess what — Mr. Parkin says someone's been stealing fruit and stuff from the storeroom. He was wondering who it could be, but now he thinks it must have been Charlie."

"That means he's staying close to the farm," said Sam. "As long as he's hungry, he won't go far away. Come on, Clare."

The two girls started up the path toward the woods, Jovan went with Matthew to search the barn, and Katie set off by herself.

Behind the milking shed was a steep bank covered with brambles and young willow trees. There was no real path. She had to pull herself up the bank by hanging onto branches, and once she grabbed hold of a bramble bush by mistake. She began to wish she'd gone with one of the others. And yet she felt certain she was right; this was the most obvious place to look for Charlie. He would surely stay close to Marsh Farm, where he knew there was food to be found and shelter at night, perhaps in one of the barns. After being lost for so long he must be feeling scared.

Something made a loud whirring noise overhead. She froze, then saw it was only a big black crow taking off with a noisy flapping of wings. But what could have startled it?

"Charlie," she called, but in a whisper. "Charlie, are you there?"

No reply.

Her hand hurt where she had grabbed the brambles. She looked down and saw that it was bleeding slightly. Soon it would be dark. If only she could hear a shout from the others to say that they had found him. Then she could give up and go back . . .

THWACK!

A branch came hurtling down, missing her by inches. She leaped back in alarm and stared up into the trees. She couldn't see anything . . . but then, it wouldn't be easy to detect a small brown monkey in the tangle of branches. The willows would provide him with a natural camouflage.

"Charlie?" she called, louder than before. "Is that you?"

THWACK!

Another branch came hurtling down. This time it struck a glancing blow on her shoulder.

"Now listen, Charlie," she said firmly. "There's no need to attack me. I'm only trying to help . . ."

THWACK!

She began to feel annoyed. "Charlie, will you please stop throwing things and come down from that tree! Fran will be here soon . . ."

"Katie? Katie, where are you?"

It was her father's voice. She could hear him coming toward her, crashing through the undergrowth. "Dad, sssh!" she pleaded. "You'll frighten him."

"Ah, there you are!" He appeared, looking hot and bothered. "I came to tell you, Sam thinks she's found the monkey

in the woods. And that girl from the sanctuary has just arrived. She's gone straight there to try and catch him."

"No!" said Katie. "Sam's wrong. Charlie's here, up in the trees. He's been throwing sticks at me."

Dad peered up at the branches. "I can't see anything . . ."

Katie groaned. "I bet you frightened him off, making all that noise! Come on, we'd better get Fran."

Chapter 9

Sizzling Sausages

"I'm *sure* it was Charlie I heard," Sam told Fran. "It was a sort of chattering noise, very fast, like this . . ." She made a clicking sound with her tongue.

"*I* think it was a woodpecker," said Clare.

Sam ignored her. "And something was moving around, right up there . . ."

She pointed into the branches of a tall oak tree.

Fran peered upward. "If you stay very quiet, I'll try calling him again." She raised her voice. "Charlie? Charlie, can you hear me? You're perfectly safe. I'm here to take you home . . ."

Sam held her breath. Everything seemed hushed in the woods. No chattering noise, no movement in the oak tree. Just the three of them, crouched and silent, and the faintest whisper of leaves.

Clare said obstinately, "I still think it was a woodpecker."

Fran sighed. "Well, he doesn't seem to be here now. He'd have come when I called, I know he would."

She looked so disheartened that Sam felt guilty for raising her hopes. Oh, how she wished Charlie would come swinging down from the trees and prove Clare wrong!

Voices came toward them — Katie and her father. Katie's sounded high and argumentative. "But Dad, it couldn't possibly have been a bird. Birds don't throw sticks —"

She stopped short when she saw Fran.

Her father said, "Katie thinks Charlie's in the trees behind the milking shed. I told her that Sam had already seen him here in the woods, but —"

"Did you say he threw sticks?" Fran interrupted.

"Yes, he did!" said Katie indignantly. "One of them actually hit me."

Fran's eyes lit up. "Throwing sticks is typical monkey behavior. It means he was frightened and trying to warn you off. Can you take me to the exact spot where it happened?"

They set off down the path, Katie leading the way and Fran close behind.

"Too bad, Sam," said Katie's dad. "Looks like you must have been mistaken. Never mind, at least you tried." He followed the others.

Sam and Clare looked at each other. Clare said, "I did tell you —"

"Yeah, yeah, it was only a woodpecker," snapped Sam. "Come on, let's go and see if they find him."

Everyone wanted to join in the search, but Fran said it was best if she and Katie went alone. Too many people would scare Charlie even more.

Matthew, Jovan, Sam, and Clare sat on the wall in the yard, waiting. "It'll

be dark soon," said Jovan gloomily. "They'll never find him now."

Sam felt really, really fed up. She had wanted so badly to be the one who found Charlie, but instead she'd messed things up by insisting he was in the woods when all the time he'd been hiding in the trees behind the milking shed. And now they'd lost valuable time and it was all her fault.

"My parents say monkeys are dangerous animals," said Clare. "They're scared he might hurt the baby. They say they'd never have come here if they'd known about the animal sanctuary being so close."

At last Fran and Katie returned. "No sign of him," said Fran despairingly. "And I'll have to get back to the sanctuary soon. There's just one last thing we could try . . ."

"What's that?" asked Matthew.

"Charlie adores sausages. If we were to cook some over an open fire he might be tempted to join us, especially if he's hungry."

"We could have a barbecue!" Sam felt better at once. She would much rather be *doing* something than just hanging around. Besides, she loved barbecues.

"I'll ask my brother to set it up," said Fran. "The best place would be right here in the yard. Then, if Charlie's anywhere near the farm, he'll be able to smell the cooking." She started toward the farmhouse.

"I hate barbecues," said Clare. "Rotten old burned sausages — ugh!"

"Oh, you hate everything!" snapped Katie.

Clare went white, and when Mr. Parkin

appeared carrying a portable grill, she stomped off. They didn't see her for the rest of the evening.

Nor, sadly, did they see Charlie, even though the sausages sizzling in the pan filled the air with the most tempting smells imaginable. When it grew dark, Fran said she couldn't stay any longer. She was too worried about the other animals at the sanctuary.

"If you want to come back tomorrow morning I'll petsit for you," said Jovan. "You know, answer the telephone and all that."

"Will you really?" Fran looked relieved. "That would be a big help."

"I'll go with him," said Sam, who still felt guilty about misleading Fran earlier. She explained, "We always petsit in pairs in case there are any problems."

Fran said goodnight to everyone and hurried away. Reluctantly, they doused the fire and went indoors, but not before Sam had wrapped a sausage in a paper napkin and stuffed it into her jeans pocket. *Might come in handy*, she thought.

Back in her room, she wrote a postcard to her father:

Dear Dad,

You'll never guess what's happened! Mr. Parkin's sister Fran — she runs an animal sanctuary — has lost a monkey called Charlie, so we're helping her look for him. We think he's here at the farm because Clare Spencer-Brown saw a face at the window. And he threw sticks at Katie so last night we

Here she ran out of space and had to continue on a second postcard:

By the time she had finished, Clare and

...had a barbecue because we hoped Charlie would smell sausages. But he didn't. Jo and I are going to petsit at the sanctuary so that Fran can search again. Hope you are well.
Don't forget to eat
Love Sam x ☺

Katie had gone to bed. Sam washed and undressed, turned out the light and climbed onto her bunk.

For a long time she tossed and turned, unable to sleep. It was a warm night and the room seemed unbearably stuffy. Then she remembered that Katie had insisted they keep the windows closed.

Sam understood her concern for Archie's safety, but with no air coming into the room they could die of suffocation! Surely, if she opened the window above the empty top bunk, Archie wouldn't be in danger, would he?

Cautiously, she got out of bed. Both Katie and Clare were sound asleep. She could hear their soft, regular breathing. She climbed the ladder to the empty top bunk and crawled toward the window. Slowly, carefully, she eased it open. Fresh air came drifting in, cooling her hot face. Whew, that was better! She climbed back down the ladder and into bed.

She fell asleep almost at once. When she woke up, it was morning.

The first thing she noticed was the paper napkin lying on the floor. She stooped to pick it up, wondering where it could have come from. Then she remembered she had used it to wrap up the sausage last night. She felt in her jeans pocket . . .

Nothing there!

"What are you doing?" asked a sleepy voice.

Sam swung around to see Clare sitting up in bed, rubbing her eyes. "Did you eat my sausage?" she demanded.

"What?"

"There was a sausage in my pocket last night. Did you eat it?"

"Course not!" Clare looked disgusted. "I told you, I hate burned sausages."

"Well, somebody did . . ." Sam climbed the ladder and shook Katie's hunched shoulder. "Katie, wake up! Did you eat my sausage?"

Katie groaned and buried her head in the pillow.

Sam looked across at the other top bunk. She saw the open window . . . and the blanket all rumpled . . . and a couple of discarded banana skins . . .

"Charlie!" she breathed.

Katie sat up with a start. "Where?"

"Oh, he's not here now. At least, I don't think he is." Sam checked under the bunks and looked in the bathroom. "No, he's gone. But I think that's who it was. I'll bet he smelled the sausage and came in through the open window. And he must have stolen some more bananas from the storeroom, because he's left the skins all over the top bunk."

Clare gasped. "You mean he slept here last night — in the room with us?"

"Looks like it. The blanket's all rumpled."

Katie uttered a loud and anguished wail. "Archie!" She reached for the cockroach's box and opened the lid. "Oh, my dear — you're safe! I was afraid —"

"Don't worry about Archie." Sam started pulling on her clothes. "This is urgent. We have to tell the others right away. And one of us had better call Fran . . ."

Chapter 10

"I Hate This Place!"

It was Jovan who called Fran and told her about the missing sausage and the banana skins. He wanted to go and petsit at the sanctuary first thing, but Mrs. Parkin insisted he have some breakfast first. He sat at the long table with the others, eating as fast as he could. The sooner Fran could be free to come and find Charlie the better, as far as he was concerned!

"Katie, what's Archie's box doing on the table?" asked her mother. "Cockroaches aren't welcome at mealtime. You should have left him in your room."

"No way!" Katie said grimly. "Not while Charlie's on the loose. It's a wonder poor Archie's still alive after *somebody* opened a window last night." She glared at Sam.

Matthew grinned. "I don't know what you're worried about," he said. "If Charlie's got a taste for sausages, he's not likely to go after Archie. There isn't a lot of meat on a cockroach."

Katie looked horrified. Her mother said quickly, "At least put his box on the floor."

After a while, Clare came into the dining room. She looked pale and upset.

"Where are your parents?" asked Mrs. Parkin.

"They're having an argument." Clare sat down at the other table by herself.

"You can come and sit with us, if you want," said Matthew.

"No, thanks."

There was an awkward pause, then everyone continued eating and talking about nothing in particular. Everyone, that is, except Sam, who seemed rather quiet.

Eventually she said, "Jo, would you mind very much if I didn't come petsitting with you this morning? Because I'd really like to be here when Fran comes. I want to help her find Charlie more than anything."

Jovan shrugged. "It doesn't matter, as long as there are two of us. Matthew can come with me instead."

Matthew's face fell. "Mr. Parkin said he'd be giving Ben another lesson this morning. But if you need —"

"I'll do it," Clare said unexpectedly. "I'll help Jovan."

"But you're not a Petsitter!" said Katie. "We're the experts. It says so in our ad."

Clare went pink. "I'm an expert, too." She stood up. "I'll tell my parents."

When she'd gone, Sam said, "I suppose she means she's an expert on horses. You'll have to watch her, Jo. Don't let her go anywhere near Major."

"I won't," he promised.

He had decided to take Hammy with him. Charlie might not be interested in a cockroach, but a plump little hamster could be far more tempting, and he didn't want to take any chances. He picked up the cage and met Clare in the yard.

Together they set off for the sanctuary.

"The animals have already been fed," Fran told them when they arrived at her office. "All you need to do is answer the phone and keep an eye on things generally. By the way, last night I told the police that Charlie's missing. They'll probably call this morning to ask if I've found him yet. You'd better tell them he's been seen near Marsh Farm."

"Okay," said Jovan.

When Fran had gone, he made room for Hammy's cage on the desk. Clare sat in the chair. "You haven't asked why my parents were arguing," she said.

"I didn't think it was any of my business," said Jovan.

Clare pursed up her mouth. "When I told my mom the monkey was in our room last night, she said she wanted to go home right away. But my dad said leaving now would be a waste of money. She said if it wasn't found soon she'd start packing. That's why they were arguing."

"What about you?" Jovan asked. "You don't seem to be enjoying yourself much. Do *you* want to go home?"

"I don't really care." She stood up. "I think I'll go and see the ponies."

"All right," said Jovan. "But you'd better not try to ride that nervous one. What's his name?"

"Major. Don't worry, I'm good with horses. Everyone says so." Clare marched out of the office.

Jovan settled down to read the hamster article he had started yesterday. After about ten minutes, the telephone rang.

"Hello," said a female voice. "Is this the animal sanctuary?"

"Yes, it is," he said. "Can I help you?"

"I hear you've lost a monkey."

"Well . . . yes, but — Are you the police?" The voice mumbled something he couldn't hear. "So it's on the loose and you don't have any idea where it is?"

"Not exactly," said Jovan. "We know it's somewhere near Marsh Farm because it came indoors last night. It stole a sausage and slept on a bunk in one of our bedrooms. But by this morning it had gone again."

"Really? At Marsh Farm, did you say?"

"Yes, that's where we're staying." Jovan thought he'd better explain. "I'm only looking after the sanctuary while Fran's over at the farm, searching for Charlie. That's the monkey. We're Petsitters, you

see, so we're used to taking care of animals."

"Did you say Petsitters?"

"Yes, there are four of us altogether. We're all members of the Petsitters Club and we've come to Marsh Farm for a vacation."

"And your names are . . .?"

"I'm Jovan, and the others are Samantha, Matthew, and Katie. Actually, Matthew and Katie's dad is a policeman. He's staying at the farm too, so if you need his help —" The line went dead. Jovan replaced the receiver. What a strange telephone call! She didn't sound a bit like a policewoman. But who was she?

And where was Clare? She'd been gone ages. *You'll have to watch her*, Sam had warned. *Don't let her go anywhere near Major . . .*

Jovan sighed. He didn't want to leave the telephone unmanned, but he supposed he'd better make sure Clare wasn't doing anything stupid. Besides, he'd promised himself he'd go to see the donkey. He liked donkeys. Sometimes he went to a local sanctuary to visit Dillon, the little gray donkey he had once helped to rescue.

"I won't be long," he told the sleeping Hammy. "And I'll close the door behind me, just in case."

When he reached the paddock, he saw Clare inside the fence, standing close to Major and whispering in his ear. "No!" he called out, horrified. "Get away! Leave him alone!"

Startled, the chestnut reared back, flattening his ears and showing the whites of his eyes. With a snort, he wheeled around and galloped off to the far side of the paddock, scattering the other ponies in his path.

Clare turned toward Jovan, her face scarlet. "You idiot! He was just beginning to trust me and now you've scared him off. Why did you have to start yelling like that?"

"I thought you were going to ride him," said Jovan.

"Do you think I'm crazy? Look!" She spread her empty hands wide. "No bridle, no saddle. I was only trying to make friends with him, that's all."

"Well, I'm sorry," said Jovan. "But it's a big responsibility, looking after the sanctuary. I didn't want to take any risks."

"Oh, you all think you're so wonderful, don't you?" She glared at him furiously.

"You and your famous Petsitters Club! Well, you may be experts on hamsters and cockroaches, but I bet you don't know as much as I do about ponies."

Jovan began to feel embarrassed. "Maybe not, but—"

"I keep saying I'm good with horses, but nobody seems to believe me." Clare's chin began to wobble. "You don't like me, that's what it is. And do you want to know something funny? When we heard there'd be another family staying here, my dad said, 'That's good. You'll be able to make friends with them.' Hah! You're the most unfriendly bunch I've ever met."

"That's not true!" said Jovan. "We did try —"

"My mom said she knew this wasn't the kind of vacation I wanted, but it was the best they could manage while Simon's still a baby. And at least I'd have other kids to play with." Clare's face crumpled. "The stupid thing is that I was really looking forward to it. But it's turned out to be the worst vacation I've ever had in my life."

Jovan stared at her, unable to think of anything to say.

"I *hate* this place. I wish I'd never come here. I want to go home!" She burst into tears.

Chapter 11

"Quick — Get a Picture!"

Dear Dad,
I know I'm using up all
my Postcards but last night
CHARLIE SLEPT ON OUR TOP BUNK!
We Know because he stole a sausage
from my jeans Pocket. And he left
banana skins lying around. But in the
morning he'd gone. So now Fran's here
searching for him again. I hope we
find him Soon! Hope you are well.
Love Sam × ☺   P.s Don't forget to eat!

Just as she finished writing, Matthew came in. "Hello," said Sam, surprised. "I thought you were going to watch Ben having another lesson."

"Mr. Parkin said we'd better wait until Charlie's been found." Matthew sat down gloomily beside her. "So I could have gone with Jovan after all. Now I feel bad about it. Somehow, I don't think Clare will be much good as a petsitter."

"I feel bad too," Sam admitted. "The trouble is that part of me wanted to go to the sanctuary to see the ponies again, but most of me wanted to stay here. I couldn't bear to miss the moment when Fran finds Charlie at last."

"If she ever does." Matthew sighed. "A policeman's just arrived to help. He and Dad have gone up to search the area around the pond."

Sam shook her head. "Charlie's closer than that, I *know* he is."

Matthew stood up. "I think I'll go over to the sanctuary and make sure Jo's okay. Mom's going down to the village soon. Shall I ask her to mail that card for you?"

"Yes, please." She gave him all three postcards, including the two she had written last night.

When he'd gone, she remained sitting on her bunk, thinking about Clare. In some ways she seemed so lucky, especially owning her own pony; but in others she didn't seem lucky at all. It was a shame she was so stuck-up. If she'd been different, they might have found it easier to make friends with her . . .

What was that?

Sam looked around the room, certain she had heard something. A little low moaning noise, barely audible. But did it come from inside the room . . . or outside? She held her breath, listening hard.

There it was again!

It was inside the room, she felt sure. And somewhere high. Cautiously, she stood up to get a better view.

At first she could see nothing. She glanced at the window above the empty bunk and saw that it was still open. Beneath it the blanket was rumpled, but she had taken the banana skins away before breakfast to show Mrs. Parkin. In fact, now that she thought about it, she had also straightened the blanket . . .

So how had it become rumpled again?

Again she heard the moaning sound. This time she felt certain it came from the top bunk. She crept closer.

Was it her imagination, or could she see a little shape curled up against the pillow? A shape with eyes and ears . . . and fingers . . . and a long curly tail. . .

"Charlie?" she whispered.

The shape moved. A small monkey face stared back at her. He puckered up his mouth and gave another plaintive moan.

Sam knew she must be very, very careful. One false move and she might scare him into flight. If only she could close the window . . . but she couldn't reach it without stretching past him.

On the other hand, if she left him alone while she went to fetch Fran, he might disappear again . . .

"Hello, Charlie dear," she said in her most soothing voice. "My name's Sam, and I'm a friend of Fran's. She's out looking for you now."

He watched her warily, his round eyes anxious.

Sam went on, "I'm not really a stranger, you know. It was my sausage you stole last night. And it was me sleeping in the bottom bunk. So we do sort of know each other already."

He puckered up his mouth again and made a little kissing movement toward her with his lips.

"You can trust me, Charlie. I won't hurt you. I only want to help you." Slowly and carefully she reached toward him. "Please, *please* let me help you."

He hesitated, then put out a cautious finger to touch her hand. He snatched it right back. But she held her hand steady, leaving it there for him to touch if he wanted.

At last he found the courage to try again.

This time, he gripped her finger and pulled it toward his mouth. For a minute she thought he was going to bite it, but he only held her hand against his lips. Then he began to rock gently to and fro, moaning quietly.

"Oh, Charlie!" she breathed "What's the matter? Are you in pain?"

Behind her the door swung open. "Sam?" said Katie's voice. "Do you want to come and —?"

"Ssssh!" she hissed without turning around. "Be quiet or you'll frighten him."

"Frighten who?"

"Charlie. He's here on the top bunk, holding my hand. But I think there's something wrong with him." The little monkey hadn't moved. He sat with his sad brown eyes fixed on her face.

Katie took a step forward. "Let me look —"

"No! Don't come any closer," Sam warned. "Quick, go and get Fran."

"But I want to see —"

"You'll see him soon enough. Just do as I say."

Still Katie hesitated.

"Hurry up!" urged Sam. "I'm scared he'll try to escape through the window."

But Charlie showed no sign of wanting to escape. When Katie had gone, he continued to rock backward and forward, gripping Sam's finger so tightly it hurt. She kept on talking to him in a low, soothing voice.

"I bet you came looking for another sausage, didn't you? Fran says you love sausages. We had a barbecue last night, especially for you. We hoped you'd smell it and come a little closer, but you didn't. I suppose there were too many people around."

As soon as she stopped talking he looked anxious, so she began again. She told him all about the Petsitters Club and the animals they'd taken care of and the funny things that had happened to them.

"My dad would love to draw you, Charlie. He's an artist, you see, and he often puts our adventures into his comic strip. He won't believe it when I tell him about you. I'll have to send him another postcard . . ."

Behind her the door opened. A voice said quietly, "Sam, it's me — Fran. Is Charlie still here?"

"Yes, but I think he's sick." Sam didn't dare turn around. "He keeps rocking . . . and he won't let go of my finger."

Fran came to stand beside her. "Oh, Charlie!" she said softly. "You gave me such a fright. Come here, you silly boy."

At last the little monkey let go of Sam's finger. He reached out his long arms and wound them around Fran's neck, making little hoo-hoo noises of delight. She lifted him off the bunk and held him close.

"What's the matter, little one?" she murmured into his ear. "Have you got a tummy-ache?"

He hugged her tightly, hoo-hooing as if he was trying to tell her everything that had happened to him in the last forty-eight hours.

"Poor Charlie." Sam stroked the hairy little hand clutching at Fran's collar. "Don't worry, you're safe now. You're going home."

Fran said, "I think I'd better take him to the vet first and have him checked over. My guess is that he's eaten something that's upset him, probably some sort of poisonous leaves. He doesn't have much sense where food is concerned, I'm afraid."

"He's not going to die, is he?" asked Sam, alarmed. "He'll get better, won't he?"

"Yes, but he may need a shot. Do you think Jovan will mind taking care of the sanctuary a while longer?"

"Don't worry about Jo," said Sam. "He'll be okay. Please — could I come with you to the vet?"

"If you want. We'll ask Tom to drive, so that you and I can sit in the back with Charlie." At the door Fran hesitated. "I must warn you, there's a reporter outside. She seems to have found out about the Petsitters Club, I don't know how. And she's brought a photographer."

A small crowd awaited them in the yard — Mr. and Mrs. Parkin, Mr. and Mrs. Spencer-Brown with the baby, Matthew's dad with a policeman in uniform, Katie (still holding Archie's box), a woman with a notebook, and a man with a camera.

"There they are!" exclaimed the woman. "And they've got the monkey with them. Quick — get a picture . . ."

Chapter 12

"We're Going to be Famous!"

Meanwhile, Matthew was on his way to the sanctuary. When he arrived, he went straight to Fran's office, but found it empty apart from Hammy, asleep in his cage on the desk. He was about to go in search of Jovan when the telephone rang.

"Hello, is this the animal sanctuary?" asked a man's voice.

"Er . . . yes," said Matthew. "But I'm afraid there's nobody —"

"Are you one of the kids? The — er, Petwatchers."

"If you mean the Petsitters, yes I am," said Matthew, surprised.

"Oh, good. Have you found the monkey yet?"

"No, Fran's still looking for him. Did you want —?"

"Stay there. We'll send a crew over right away." The line went dead.

Puzzled, Matthew replaced the receiver.

Jovan appeared in the doorway, panting hard. "I thought I heard the phone . . ."

"You did," said Matthew. "But it was only some guy talking about a crew. Jo, are you all right?"

"Yeah. Why?"

"You look stressed out." Matthew confessed, "Actually, I felt bad about leaving you to take care of the sanctuary alone. That's why I came —"

He broke off as Clare appeared behind Jovan. Her eyes looked pink and puffy, as if she'd been crying.

"You didn't need to worry," said Jovan. "I wasn't alone. I had Clare to help me."

"Er, yes," said Matthew. "But I thought   "

Jovan added quickly, "She's great with horses. You should see her. She's got Major eating out of her hand."

Clare managed a watery smile. "You just have to win their confidence," she said. "I love horses more than anything in the world."

Matthew stared at her in amazement.

It was the first time he'd ever heard her say that she loved something rather than hating it. And she looked much less grumpy than usual.

"I've told her she can be a Petsitter, just for this vacation," said Jovan. "She can't be a regular member because she lives too far away, but she's going to try to start her own Petsitters Club at home."

"I know two people I can ask right away," Clare said eagerly. "And when my baby brother's old enough, he can join the club, too."

"Oh . . . good." Matthew didn't know quite what to say.

Clare said, "I think I'll go back to the paddock now. Major's probably wondering where I've gone." She left the room.

Jovan peered into the cage as if to

reassure himself that Hammy was safe. "I won't be happy until they catch that monkey," he muttered.

"You're as bad as the Spencer-Browns." Matthew looked outside the door to check that Clare had really gone. "Hey, Jo — what's happened to her? She seems like a different person, much nicer than she was before."

"Yeah, she's okay." Jovan lowered his voice. "Actually she got pretty upset and told me everything. I think she felt a bit left out, that's all. That's why I said she could be a member of the Petsitters Club."

Matthew frowned. "As long as she doesn't do anything stupid, like trying to ride that pony again without Fran's permission."

"She won't, she gave me her word. And she really is good with horses, you know.

She seems to have a special way of talking to them. That horse looked really nervous, but she managed to calm him down just by whispering in his ear. After five minutes he was ready to follow her anywhere. I'd never have believed it if I hadn't seen it with my own eyes." Jovan sat down behind the desk and picked up a notebook. "Who did you say telephoned?"

"He didn't give a name. He just said I should stay here and he was sending a crew over. But he didn't say what kind of a crew."

Jovan sighed. "That's the second strange telephone call . . ."

He broke off as Katie burst into the room, hot and panting.

"I came to tell you — Charlie's been found!" she gasped. "But he's got a stomach-ache, so Fran's taken him to the vet and Sam's gone with her. Then they're coming back here."

"Oh, good," said Matthew. "That means we can —"

"That's not all," Katie interrupted. "There's a reporter coming to take our picture. She wants all the Petsitters together, so she can put us in the newspaper. We're going to be famous!"

By the time Fran and Sam got back, the reporter was waiting for them, together with her photographer. They took pictures of Fran getting out of the back of the car, followed by Sam, with Charlie clinging around her neck. Matthew, Jovan, and Katie tried to get closer, but the reporter pushed them aside.

"Is the monkey all right?" she asked.

"What did the vet say?"

"The vet says he's going to be fine," said Fran. "All he needs now is some peace and quiet. So if you don't mind —"

"Are you going to put him back with the other monkeys? Can we get a picture of them playing together?"

"Not yet," Fran said firmly. "Now, if you'll excuse us . . ." She started toward the house.

"What about the kids?" called the reporter. "The Petsitters Club. Have they been helpful?"

Fran stopped. "Yes, they've been wonderful. Absolutely wonderful. I don't know how I'd have managed without them."

"Can we have a picture, please? The kids with the monkey."

Fran hesitated. Then she said, "Oh, all right. But don't take too long."

The photographer waved the other Petsitters over and started arranging them for a photograph. "The girl with the monkey in the middle," he said. "The boys on either side of her, and the little girl in the front."

"What does he mean — *little* girl?" said Katie indignantly.

"You want to be seen, don't you?" Matthew said with a grin. He caught sight of Clare hovering by the gate. "Hi, Clare!" he called. "You're a Petsitter, too. Come and be in the photograph."

Looking awkward but pleased, Clare joined the group.

Matthew saw Sam's look of surprise. "I'll explain later," he muttered in her ear.

The photographer crouched in front of them and started clicking away. Charlie hid his face against Sam's neck.

"I think he likes me," she whispered to Matthew. "Fran says I can help her at the sanctuary for the rest of the vacation. She says we all can, if we want."

Matthew was about to say he'd rather help Mr. Parkin train Ben when a van pulled up and three people jumped out. The first carried a clipboard, the second a hand-held camera, and the third had a thick furry microphone on a long pole.

"Hi," said the girl with the clipboard. "We're the TV crew. We've come to film the kids with the monkey . . ."

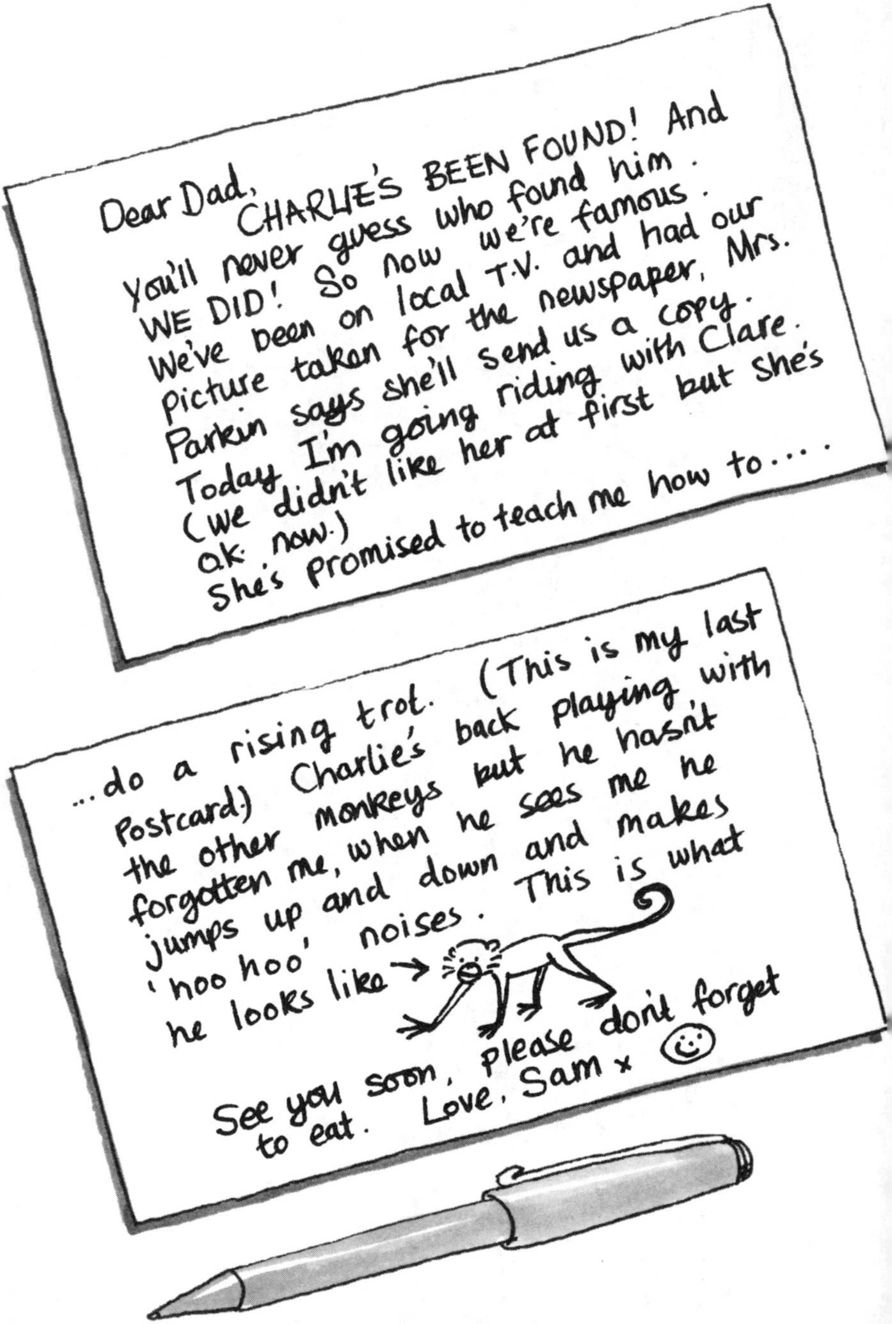
Dear Dad,
CHARLIE'S BEEN FOUND! And
you'll never guess who found him.
WE DID! So now we're famous.
We've been on local T.V. and had our
picture taken for the newspaper, Mrs.
Parkin says she'll send us a copy.
Today I'm going riding with Clare.
(we didn't like her at first but she's
ok now.)
She's promised to teach me how to....
...do a rising trot. (This is my last
Postcard.) Charlie's back playing with
the other monkeys but he hasn't
forgotten me, when he sees me he
jumps up and down and makes
'hoo hoo' noises. This is what
he looks like →
See you soon, please don't forget
to eat. Love, Sam x

Join the Petsitters Club for *more* animal adventure!

Look out for: